CAN YOU YAWN LIKE A FAWN?

MONICA SWEENEY

with Certified Pediatric Sleep Consultant **LAUREN YELVINGTON**

Illustrated by **LAURA WATKINS**

**ST. MARTIN'S
CASTLE POINT**

NEW YORK

www.stmartins.com

The Library of Congress Cataloging-in-Publication Data is available upon request

ISBN 978-1-250-10416-8 (hardcover)

Our books may be purchased in bulk for promotional, educational,
or business use. Please contact your local bookseller or the Macmillan Corporate
and Premium Sales Department at (800) 221-7945, extension 5442, or by e-mail
at MacmillanSpecialMarkets@macmillan.com.

First Edition: February 2016

10 9 8 7 6 5 4 3 2

Cover and book design by Claire MacMaster, barefoot art graphic design

CAN YOU
YAWN
LIKE A FAWN?

The Help-Your-Child-to-Sleep Method

IMAGINE A STORY that can actually help your little one relax and calm their bodies so that they can fall asleep more easily! *Can You Yawn Like a Fawn?* is designed to help parents streamline the sometimes challenging process of getting their child to sleep. While your little one is immersed in the illustrations and the story, you'll notice the clinical strategies at work in the text. Repetition of key phrases, soothing and suggestive language, and the encouragement of bedtime actions like stretching and yawning are there to support you in the effort to relax your child to sleep.

Reading stories should be a great way to bond with our children as we snuggle up before bedtime, but they are also an effective cue that the time for sleep is coming soon. Set the stage for bedtime one hour in advance. As you prepare to incorporate *Can You Yawn Like a Fawn?* into your bedtime routine, take stock of your regular routine and consider implementing a sleep-enhancing sequence.

The Sleep-Enhancing Sequence

» Turn off electronics to reduce visual stimulation and allow an increase in melatonin—the body's natural sleep aid!

» Give your child a bath

» Draw the shades

» Turn on white noise machines

» Dim the lights

Now that you have prepared a healthy bedtime routine for your child, cuddle up and yawn along with the sleepy characters in *Can You Yawn Like a Fawn?* For every word in bold, there is a sleepy action to perform with your child. For every yawn in italics, draw the word out in a soothing voice. Use your child's name in the story as you ask them if they can yawn along with the drowsy characters. As the story goes on and you read calmly and slowly, your child will feel the suggestive effects of yawning with each of the animals, and ready themselves for sleep with bedtime actions like stretching and getting cozy. *Can You Yawn Like a Fawn?* will make bedtime reading a peaceful and positive way to get your child to sleep.

—*Lauren Yelvington, Certified Child Sleep Consultant*

All around the world,
all the little animals
are going to sleep.

Down in the South Pole,
    baby penguin waddles,
        slips, and slides his little feet to bed.
All burrowed in, he **calms** his flippers
        and he *yawns* a shivery yawn.

Can you *yawn* like a penguin?

In the land down under,
   silly kangaroo hops and hops
      until she has hopped herself out, *phew*!
She **snuggles** into bed
   and *yawns* a happy yawn.

Can you *yawn* like a kangaroo?

In the prairie, teeny mouse
scurries to her tiny house.
She **droops** her sleepy head,
squeaks a tiny squeak,
and *yawns* a tiny yawn.

Can you *yawn* like a mouse?

In the desert, little lion has roared
all his roars for the day.
He **curls up** in a ball,
puffs up his chest
and *yawns* a BIG yawn.

Can you *yawn* like a lion?

On the pond,
   little ducky paddles her feet,
      splish-splash, all the way to shore.
She **flops** into her nest
   and *yawns* a quacky yawn.

Can you *yawn* like a ducky?

In the great wide river,
happy hippo is all tuckered out.
When he **relaxes** on the ground,
he opens his mouth as wide as can be
and *yawns* a low and slow yawn.

Can you *yawn* like a hippo?

In the woods,
   furry fawn is ready for a nap.
With a swish of her tail and a crinkle
   of her nose, she **nestles** into the grass
   and *yawns* a sweet yawn.

Can you *yawn* like a fawn?

In the green grove,
    drowsy panda chews softly
        on his bamboo.
He **slumps** on over and
    yawns a snoring yawn.

Can you *yawn*
    like a panda?

In the grasslands, sleepy elephant
drifts in and out of slumber.
Stretching from his toes to his trunk,
he *yawns* a dreamy yawn.

Can you *yawn* like an elephant?

Out on the farm,
   fluffy lamb can't keep her eyes open.
She **cuddles** next to mama,
   and *yawns* a snuggly yawn.

Can you *yawn* like a lamb?

Under the moonlight,
  soft kitty **breathes** in and out,
    in and out.
All rolled up in a ball,
  he *yawns* a purring yawn.

Can you *yawn* like a kitty?

At the end of the bed,
    fuzzy puppy is nice and warm.
Dreaming puppy dreams,
    she *yawns* a snoozing yawn.

Can you *yawn* like a puppy?

And you are a
sleepy little animal, too.
With one last **hug**,
you're all tucked in,
from your sleepy head
to your sleepy toes.

Can you *yawn* a goodnight yawn?